THE URBAN EROTICA
FAIRY TALE COLLECTION

I0583940

THE URBAN EROTICA
FAIRY TALE COLLECTION

Princess Pea's Bed

Honey Cummings

4 Horsemen
Publications, Inc.

4 Horsemen
Publications, Inc.

4 Horsemen Publications, Inc.
1497 Main St. Suite 169
Dunedin, FL 34698
4horsemenpublications.com
info@4horsemenpublications.com

Cover & Typesetting by Battle Goddess Productions
Editior Vanessa Valiente

Paperback ISBN-13: 978-1-64450-116-0
Ebook ISBN-13: 978-1-64450-115-3

Party Time

Pearl Hollandale tugged at her dress, aiming for the skirt to skim her thighs enough to cover her ass. Checking her lipstick once more in the mirror, she smirked. Her birthday party was ending. She had snuck into her master bedroom to catch her breath. Granted, the possible hookups proved no different from normal. But still...

So many to flirt with, so little time left to do it in!

Leaving her bathroom, her luxury apartment was filled with guests. Her birthday fell in the middle of the week, so she decided to celebrate early and have a huge gathering. Granted, the idea wasn't her entire concept. The bartender—her close friend Michael, had coordinated and hosted the whole night. When someone had too much, he'd cut them off and call them a Guber.

I wish he'd let me pay him for his efforts. It took everything I had to have him let me pay for catering and alcohol. Still, if it weren't for him handling events, I wouldn't relax. His day job as a project manager gave him an edge.

Buzzing around, weaving around groups of guests, she checked on the remaining few, telling them good night and thanking them for their birthday wishes. The catering company had done an amazing job, preparing an assortment of finger foods to fill her entire large island counter.

Plucking a cherry from a bowl, she smiled, wanting the night to drag on as long as possible. Music thumped over the custom stereo system, not drowning out a single conversation. Yet, there were plenty of folks dancing near the living room miniature bar.

Everything is just... perfect. Michael! You know how to please a girl and treat her to a good birthday. I might have to reconsider dating you one day.

Pearl grabbed a stool from the bar, her cheeks aching from smiling as she suckled on the cherry. Her eyes took in all the happy expressions unfolding between friends, old and new.

A cocktail slid across the counter and she snorted. "I didn't ask for this." She met Michael Hardy's gaze, his smirk making him more attractive.

"But you asked me to keep the drinks coming," he countered. "Have I told you how hot you look sucking on a cherry like that?"

She winked. "Maybe a time or two."

Michael leaned against the bar top, his cologne sending goosebumps over Pearl's skin. She eyed him a moment, biting the cherry at last. They'd been friends a long time, but she hadn't considered him intimately, until tonight.

Her eyes fell to his plump lips, lingering on his toothy grin. Tilting her head, she smirked at his broad shoulders. *I've never seen him shirtless, not even once.* He had passed on every gathering that involved the beach, a pool or even a jacuzzi. Another bite of the cherry filled her taste buds as she circled back to his lips, the smile gone.

"If you keep staring at me like that any longer, I might have to kiss you, Pearl." His voice was a low grumble, making her face flush. "I don't just do this for anyone."

Is Michael making a pass at me? I mean...I don't mind, but that must be a first. Not that we haven't spoken about getting together in that way... but...

Michael always dressed to the nines, like a sexy model attending a work meeting with high-end clients. Tom Ellis could be his brother, the dark eyes and dark hair paired with a devilish smile would make any woman swoon. Granted, the clean-cut beard and pulled back ponytail promised a much wilder man, ready to give you a rawer adventure.

Sharp dressed, serious faced until he gets flirty with a girl. It seems I'm his target tonight. Go figure!

For the first time, she couldn't ignore his smile, knowing it was meant for her. And her *alone*.

"You wouldn't dare." She picked up the cocktail, drinking it while arching an eyebrow.

"What makes you say that?" He furrowed his brow, his eyes lingering on her red lips.

He's smitten with me! Exactly when did this happen? But the man is always top button fastened, long sleeves and suit pants the whole time I've known him. He can't be serious? He's more adventurous than he's ever shown me in our five year of friendship. I mean, he passed on that orgy party a while back! Even the Troll got laid that night!

Placing the drink down, she leaned in and whispered into his ear, "I think you're afraid to even go shirtless around me. You'll need to show me some skin before I take you serious."

Spinning away, she left him in a wake of her teasing. She didn't dare look back, finished her drink, then the last half of her cherry. As she prowled her hallway, she spotted Gaston. The man had muscles for an older man, and he had a strong jawline that always made her heart flutter, catching a glimpse here and there.

His back muscles made her wonder if he had competed in strong man competitions when he was younger before becoming a docile professor at the local college.

Their eyes met as she spit the cherry pit into her empty glass. "You weren't supposed to see that."

"Oh?" His blue eyes sparkled with mischief. "But what I wanted to see you tie the stem."

She spun it in her finger, a smirk forming. "I imagine you didn't mean by using my fingers."

"Not with your fingers," he echoed, arching his brows.

Pearl couldn't resist the challenge. Opening her mouth wide, she stuck out her tongue and laid the stem across the pink appendage. Gaston's blue eyes watched with great attention, his body stiffening as he took a few steps closer. She retracted the stem, then began tying the stem in her mouth.

Gaston came closer, drinking a sip of his beer as Pearl's confidence faltered. He began snickering.

She continued to flip it with the tip of her tongue, to fold and bend it to a simple knot and failed repeatedly.

"May I?" He was so close, his hand on her shoulder.

Pearl slumped her shoulders, searching his blue eyes.

He wants to kiss me. Should I? Screw it, it's my birthday. If I want to kiss all the hot guys at my party, then so be it!

In defeat, she nodded.

Gaston locked lips, deepening their kiss in an instant. Before she could respond, he had plucked the stem from her own tongue and retreated. Giving him a baffled expression, she smiled. Unlike her struggle and cheeks rumbling around, his own stayed taut. She opened her lips and he opened his own and there laid across his tongue was the knotted stem.

Pearl blinked as he plucked it with his fingers, chuckling at her expression. "My, lovely Pearl, *that* is how you knot a cherry stem." He dropped it in her empty cocktail glass to join the seed.

"Enlighten me, Professor Gaston. What would this skill say about your hidden talents?" Licking her teeth, her stare bounced from head to toe, then repeating the cycle.

Chuckling, he stared at her, those icy eyes cutting through her. "Maybe one day you'll let me into your bedroom, so I can show you. We both know you're more of a..." He leaned in, his lips close to her own. "...hands on learner."

"Let's have a taste then." Pearl locked lips with him, deepening the kiss.

The tip of his tongue pressed a line down her own, making her moan. Alcohol and cherry flavors mangling in an exotic swap of flavors. The idea of his tongue rolling over her pussy, the firm tip of his tongue teasing her clit sent shivers through her. It's was tempting, to ask him to stay after the party, but she had aimed to flirt with everyone, not settle on one for the night.

Gaston pulled away, and Pearl smiled.

Tempting, but not sold on settling.

"I can't lie." Biting her bottom lip, she started to take a few steps away. "You must be the best kisser I know."

"And always will be." He winked.

"Stop it." Pearl's face flushed, and she spun on her heel. "I need another drink. I'm sorry but private study lessons weren't on my wish list this time, Professor. Please, enjoy the party, Gaston. Surely you can find a more willing student."

"I will, and happy birthday, Pearl." He raised his beer and she waved him off.

Venturing into the kitchen, she stole another cherry for herself. One of the caterers were cleaning dishes and consolidating trays to keep the platters visually pleasing. She plucked another cherry, taking in the tattooed sleeves and bearded face.

At last, he glanced up, arching a single eyebrow. "Something wrong?" His voice was smooth and playful.

She shrugged, enjoying her cherry. "I just enjoy watching a man doing the dishes."

"What else does the birthday girl enjoy?" He rinsed a platter, reached for the next, and started scrubbing it. "Nice place you've got here, by the way."

"I enjoy this and that." She changed course, reaching for a chunk of pineapple. "You don't have to do that. I have a maid coming in the morning, you know."

"It's just habit, part of what I do." He finished rinsing the platter, then shut off the faucet. "So, what can I do for you, birthday girl?"

"Your name and number?" She smiled, slipping the pineapple into her mouth, giving a playful expression.

He laughed, shaking his head. "The name's Chuckles."

"Chuckles?"

"Yeah, and I've got a girl, so no phone number today," he confessed.

Pearl sighed, looking back towards the party. "Damn, now who to hit next?"

"Did you try the bartender?" Chuckles walked around, nodding in Michael's direction.

"Sort of..." She creased her brow in thought. "Why? You think he'll play along?"

"He's been watching your every move. Even cringed when you kissed Professor Cherry Lips over there." He laughed at her baffled expression.

Was everyone watching me with Gaston? And why would Michael care?

"Don't believe me? Go find your next mark and make sure to look in his direction." He nodded at Michael again. "He's a nice guy, you know."

"I know..." She frowned. "But what suddenly makes you an expert on him?"

"His sister bartends part-time for Red." Nudging her arm, he repeated the offer. "So, are you giving the bartender a try?"

"Is that a challenge?" Pearl abandoned her empty glass on the counter, her shield gone.

"I'll put fifty bucks on it." He sucked on his cheek with a sparkle in his eyes.

She gave a smug expression. "Fine. I'll match that wager."

This is my field, and I have the advantage. No way am I losing to a part-time bar cook who caters on the side!

The Bet

P earl scanned the party stragglers, searching for her next kissing target. At last, she settled on Axle, a coworker and a long-time friend-with-benefits. It hadn't been a secret from their group, which made her curious, *Is Michael fully aware of that arrangement?*

Hell, she had texted him about it more times than she can remember.

If money is on the table, then I'm sure to win. There's no way this will make him cringe. He knows we have a casual sexual relationship.

Axle had a sexy smile and a cute, tight ass, though shorter than Michael and Gaston. In all the years she'd known him, he'd never expressed interest in having a committed relationship (her nor any other female) and took every chance to travel at work. Regardless, under his dapper outfit was a thick muscled athlete who never missed a day at the gym. Granted, his gym partner was Michael: Axle always teased and marveled at how Michael managed to workout in long sleeves during the heat of summer.

No. There's no way I'm losing fifty bucks. Not on always-has-a-shirt-on Michael.

With a wide grin, she kept Michael in her peripheral. She caught his stolen glance and it goaded her to pick up pace. To think a caterer named Chuckles caught Michael's stares before she did!

Reaching Axle, she glided her hand over his upper arm, and like a reflex, he pulled her into him. Her body ached over the heat of it against her, remembering the way he grinded against her. The Adonis belt flexing as he tensed at his own peak, adding to the arousal rolling through her. Shaking off the wanton want, she spun so Michael had a perfect view, just behind Axle.

"Kiss me," she demanded, watching as Michael paused and stared in their direction.

"Depends." He smirked, tucking her hair behind an ear. "What's the occasion?"

"I'm trying to decipher who here's the best kisser," she announced.

"Oh?" He glanced around the party, picking out his possible competition. "And who am I competing against?"

"Professor Gaston says he's the best. Chuckles denied me. And I haven't decided on who else." She stole a glance over his shoulders. "Maybe Michael?"

Axle raised a high brow. "Michael too?" he said, mischief written across his face. "I'm in. Granted, you think he'll go for it?"

"He already implied he wanted one." Again, she gave her playful shrug.

"Then, let's have a go..."

Axle cupped her face; the kiss was simple before the forceful rush of his tongue. He was far rawer and more aggressive than even Gaston. Again, thoughts of them in the bedroom crept forward, his body heating in the wake of her arousal. Even when they fucked, Axled rode her hard and fast. A thought crossed her mind, *always in a rush to go... somewhere*

She changed the direction of the kiss and peeked over Axle's shoulder.

Pearl locked eyes with Michael, and she jolted *What a painful expression!*

18

She pulled away from Axle, seeping in anger. *How did I not notice sooner?*

"So? Who's winning?" Axle was more concerned with his stats than the confusion building on her face. "Or do you need a second kiss?"

He leaned in for a second round, but her fingers stopped his lips. "No. One attempt to impress. Now, to contestant number three."

Well, if he's truly smitten with me, the kiss will expose him.

She brushed pass Axle, and Michael panicked, taking a shot he had poured while watching them makeout. By the time she climbed back into her bar stool, he had turned away to the liquor cabinet and began organizing it.

Pearl cleared her throat; he turned, slow and unsure. His face was red, embarrassed for peeking, for cringing at her kiss with Axle. She liked this moment, seeing the stoic man, in the suit vest and tie, falter for the first time.

"Come here." She signaled for him to *come hither* with a finger. "Closer."

"What's wrong?" Michael leaned in and she grabbed his tie, yanking him forward.

Their lips pressed tight and she marveled how soft and plump his lips were compared to the others. Michael deepened the kiss, much slower than the first two as his tongue slid between their interlocked lips. A hard-metallic ball rolled between her lips, gracing her teeth, and prompting her to open wider, allowing him in, curious now.

He has a tongue piercing! What? Since when!

Michael's tongue stroked along the length of her own before circling and rubbing. Her tongue wanted to chase the piercing, her aim missing its target, unable to keep up with their unfolding cat and mouse game. He turned his head, locking lips in a new direction, exploring her mouth from a new angle.

Again, she moaned, the piercing sending an exhilarating sensation over her flesh. His tongue began to withdraw, tempting her own to give chase and she thought, *What's that curious flavor lingering on her tongue?*

Cherry-flavored vodka! Is he hoping for me to kiss him next?

She licked the length of his tongue, but, before she could proceed further, he pulled away, denying her another chance of finding his piercing. She eyed his lips, marveling how he returned to his stoic expression.

Her body buzzed with want. *What else might he be hiding under his high collar and long sleeves?*

Michael tried to pull away, but she pulled him back, wanting a second sampling, unwilling to release his tie just yet. Again, he

21

took his time playing and exploring. The heat of his hand cupped her jaw and his kissing made her hungry, her skin pebbling in goosebumps.

This time she pulled away, searching his eyes in astonishment. *He's smitten with me! Am I dreaming?*

He arched an eyebrow. "Are you going to release my tie?"

"Oh!" She let go, blinking for a moment. "Wow, I... I didn't expect that."

"The kiss?" He smirked and poured them each a shot of cherry-flavored vodka.

"Never mind." Heat rose in her cheeks and she wondered, *is my face had red?* "What's the shot for?" she asked.

"Would I be too bold to say this is my winning shot?" he teased, sliding one to her.

"A shot to the winner of the kissing contest!" Her voice caught everyone's attention still lingering at the party. "To Michael!"

The room whistled and shouted their congratulations as they took shots or drinks of their own. She caught Chuckles' smirk as he motioned with rubbing fingers, *where's my money?* Snorting, she met the Gaston's scowl who turned and left down the hall out of view. He had been too cocky, his ego taking a massive hit. Axle lipped a, *wow,* and took a swig of his lemon Whiteclaw.

Turning back to Michael, she frowned. He had gone back to messing with the liquor cabinet. "You won," she insisted.

He eyed her over his shoulder. "You didn't think I could."

"Oh, come on, Mikey," Pearl fussed, panicking. "I misjudged your ability to compete. That's all."

"Oh?" This time, he met her gaze in the cabinet mirror and smiled. "I can assure you, your impression of me isn't entirely wrong. *But* it's complicated..."

"Is that so?" She stood on her feet, squinting at him. "And will you ever dare to show me what you're hiding behind your resigned exterior, Mystery Man?"

Shrugging, he kept silent, refusing to meet her eyes again.

Flustered, she marched off towards Chuckles. He held out his palm, giggling as he awaited his bet winnings. She motioned for him to wait as she snuck into her bedroom, then returned with a hundred-dollar bill.

This time, Gaston had returned and regained his composure. *He didn't find a hook-up and spiraled back for one. Ha! Such a prideful man.*

"The bet was fifty." Chuckles tilted his head.

"Yeah, but you deserve double." She glanced back at Michael, his eyes darting elsewhere. "You saw something I've failed to see for years. Anyhow, you were right. He cringed even with Axle which he knew about..." She shook her head. "So, you earned the money. Go take your girl out to eat or something."

"Nah, I'll just buy her a new dress or some new shoes." He flipped out his wallet and slid the money in.

"That's rather specific list there, Chuckles."

"It's because she lost her shoes, then ripped her dress when..." He paused, then shook his head. "It's a long story, but I feel bad about that whole night."

She sighed. "Well, it's nearing the time for this party to close up," she said, looking at her watch.

"Where do you want the leftovers?" He thumbed behind himself.

25

"I want the cherries. So place the bowl in the fridge, I like them cold." Scanning over the other platters, she settled on, "The rest is whoever wants to take it home. Otherwise, shove it in the fridge. There's plenty of room to fit everything."

"You got it, birthday girl."

Clearing her throat, she caught the attention of the partygoers. "First off, thank you all for coming to celebrate my birthday with me. I'm overjoyed to see all my friends in one place, enjoying tasty food and great drinks. Feel free to tip the caterer, and don't forget to thank our volunteer bartender, Michael."

Again, a cacophony of whistles and clapping filled the apartment.

Marching back to the bar, she leaned into Michael's ear, saying, "I'm headed to bed. Can you see them out, then lock up afterwards?"

Nodding, he snorted. "I told you before...I would take care of setup and breakdown. I don't break my promises, Princess."

She pecked him on the cheek, and he gave her a confused expression.

"Text me when you get home safely. Thank you, this was a great idea." She turned and disappeared into the master bedroom.

Pearl touched her lips, lingering on the memory of the kisses. Her mind wandered back to Gaston's playful tongue, Axle's domineering nature, and lastly, Michael's slow, lustful kiss. He was a stark contrast from the first two, something lighter and sultry.

I wouldn't mind seeing what else he might do differently to me... if only I can remove that shirt!

Surprise

Pearl decided sleep wasn't quite on her mind. *Not yet.*

She aimed for the bathroom. Her bedroom door locked to keep intruders at bay as she left Michael to flush out the crowd. She could see Gaston trying his luck, he was bold enough to waltz in and join her in the shower or tub. A smile crested her lips as she slipped into her garden tub. Axel on the other hand, he would strip down and wait for her in bed.

Hence why, neither have a key to my place.

She slid down and dunked her head underwater. Coming up, she blew the air from her lips, slow and steady. The steam and lowlighting was calming and soothing, compared to the commotion of the dying party. The music had stopped, voices fading to silence. There was the occasional clink and clack of cups and dishes.

But one of the three does have a key to my door. Has had it for a while now.

Splashing water on her face, she wiped away the last of her makeup, letting her thoughts roam. Part of her felt the temptation of arousing desires pulling at her joints. If she hurried, she could call or text anyone to enter her bed tonight.

Shaking her head, she had planned, no, made a game of it for her own birthday amusement. *I wasn't aiming to get laid tonight.*

29

A whim of mischief hit her, and she slid down to her lips into the water. Ripples waved out, obscuring her naked body under the water's surface. Her hands snaked over her body, squeezing breasts and dipping between her thighs to play for a fleeting moment. She wanted to spend her real day having an amazing erotic night. The wild orgy had been fun, but it had made her realize something surprising in the end:

I rather be with one person. The sort of partner that would explore every part of me, to the point where they knew my body than I could ever dream. Sure, having multiple partners, back to back, was an adventure. But it felt... unsatisfying. I just want the right one, the perfect fit.

Pulling out of the tub, she inhaled deep and held it. She toweled off and at last, released it as if it were suppressing her thoughts. The dam broke, the sensations flooding as lustful memories and heartfelt desires clashed.

Her body, heart, and soul were at war with one another.

Axel is great fun, but sloppy. I mean, he fucks fast and hard. Don't get me wrong, it's amazing, but do I really want that every time? Same shit, different day. He doesn't really change it up much. In fact, I sometimes wonder if he's treating me like a cheat code on a video game: left breast, right breast, up, down, up, down, and unload.

Her reflection scowled at her. The idea of Axel's redundant sex moves was more accurate than she would ever confess. Squeezing the water from her hair, she wrapped the towel around her tiny frame. She sashayed to the bedroom door and opened it slowly. The lights had been turned off, not a soul was in view. Peering out the door further, the kitchen was empty.

She tip-toed into the dining room where the bar sat. She reached the side and before sidling behind it.

Michael appeared, standing up with two liquor bottles.

Pearl screamed.

"Shit!" He grimaced and placed the bottles on the counter before he dropped them.

"MICHAEL!" She clutched her chest, tightening her fingers on the towel, out of fear of losing it.

"I thought you called it for the night?" His eyes drifted over her, and he gave a smirk. "Did you enjoy a soak in the tub?"

Clearing her throat, Pearl countered, "You're just jealous I didn't invite you to join me."

"I would've joined you if you had said *please*. To be fair, I wasn't the only one here, hoping for an invite." He laughed and pulled the spouts from the liquor bottles and replaced them with their caps and corks.

"Oh yeah?" She slid onto the bar stool as he pulled over a few more to flip out. "And who's having a hard time leaving?"

"Gaston at first." He grabbed the hand towel for a better grip and the bottle spout popped lose after a grunt. "Then some girl with a lot of hip and ass caught his fancy and he followed her out the door."

"Good riddance." Pearl offered the cap from the pile on the counter. "Two more."

"Wait, what?" Michael's face flushed before he blinked and redirected his thoughts. "Oh, bottles. Yes, so... why do you lead him on so much, Gaston that is."

"It's just fun." She shrugged, picking up another cap. "Granted, he's not my type so it's been nothing but flirting, groping, and kissing. He's got a hardon for some professor he works with, even though she's got herself someone."

"Ah, I see." He grabbed the last two bottles. "Well, Axel wanted to hang out till you came out. I shooed him out the door. Usually you'd say something if you two were spending the night together."

"Right and I don't let him stay here. I go to his place for that sort of thing," she confessed.

"Well, Pearl. It seems I don't know you as well as I thought." Another grunt and he popped the next spout free and added it to the container.

Damn, is that a monster bicep flexing under that shirt? Wonder if he grunts like that when he starts to come? Wait, what the hell am I thinking? This is Michael! Am I out of my mind? Would he even act on it if I offered? That kiss though, and the hurt expression when I kissed Axel even though he knows that history. He's friends with both me and Axel. They must talk about it. I mean they're workout buddies and...

"...Did you hear me?" Her eyes snapped back to his, and she handed the cap to his outstretched hand. "I asked why his place and not yours?"

"Oh, that," she darted her eyes away, "I don't know if a prude like yourself could handle that answer."

He popped the last bottle, a toothy grin on his face as it brought her gaze back to him. "Want to hear what I think, Princess Pea?"

And there it is. All night I half-expected him to use that pet name for me. Granted, it's only used when we're alone, or text, or whispered to take a stab at me.

Squinting her eyes at him, she smirked. "Enlighten me, oh, prude bartender."

"He's got toys."

Opening her mouth, she stopped herself and reflected on the answer.

"Well? Princess?" Capping the last bottle, he began putting them away and stealing glances through the mirror once again. "Am I right? Old Axel has quite the toy box of playthings, doesn't he? Hmm? A treasure trove of pleasure you don't have here in your castle, no?"

"You can't tell anyone" She covered her face, defeated.

You asshole, Axel! You told him! You do talk about it!

"Why not get your own?" He marveled.

"It's embarrassing and I don't know what to click on," she hissed. "How do you know he has toys?"

He laughed. "A guy as sexually active as him needs a truckload of dildos to keep up with that many libidos coming through his revolving door." Spinning back to her, he leaned across the table. "And he's told me a story or two, matching with our texts, it wasn't hard to figure out who he was talking about. No names. He's at least that trustworthy."

Regular Sherlock Holmes, aren't we?

Sliding off the bar stool, she huffed, "Why haven't you gone home, then?"

"I thought I'd be gone by now, but this took longer to undo than I thought." He motioned to the bar before wiping off the counter. "I must return the spouts to my sister since I borrowed them from her boss at Red's Tavern."

"Fine." She turned for her bedroom door. "I'm going to bed, so don't forget to lock up."

"I have a key, so..." His voice almost came out like a purr over that fact.

"Don't you dare tell anyone about that," she said, hiding behind her bedroom door, fingers tight on the towel.

I'm out of my mind!

A few minutes passed before she heard her front door shut at last. She could breathe again, part of her wanting Michael to give chase and circle back. A laugh escaped her, covering her face over the fact he pinned her for her toy fetish. She had been too afraid to buy or bring home anything. The idea of the playthings made her pussy wet.

Dammit, I can't fall asleep if I'm feeling this horny. I hate you for even bringing it up, Mikey!

4

Sleepless

Pearl clambered onto her bed, abandoning the towel on the floor. She laid back on her silken sheets, her pillows piled high on her pillowtop mattress. Closing her eyes, she let her hands glide over her breasts and across her abdomen. In her mind, she had herself a reverse harem with all the goods.

Her fingers dipped between her thighs, rubbing the opening of her pussy. *I'm so wet... just thinking about...*

Her mind shifted as her slick finger slid up and circled her clit. The pleasure and rise it brought her only fueled the erotic imagination fueling her unrestrained desires. Gaston's tongue played with her pussy, licking and diving in and out, twirling her into knots like that cherry stem. The same hard precise pressure against her tongue she now imagined sliding across her most sensitive of places, wondering how much more enjoyable it would be to roll over her swollen jewel.

Sliding one hand back up, she gripped her breast. Squeezing and pinching her nipple, she arched as she continued to play. Axel would use his teeth or nipple clamps from time to time. It drove her wild, made her drip till her thighs ran wet with her arousal.

She could feel the building buzz of her body, the rising orgasm nearing its peak. *Almost... there...*

The imagery in her mind shifted, and once more, she could feel and taste Michael's kiss. Every part of that kiss said, *let's take our time and play on the edge of pleasure.* Her breath caught, a haunting cherry flavor catching her by surprise. Arching, she was *so close, a little more... a little...*

"Dammit!" She sat up and glared at her mattress in betrayal.

Scooting off the edge, she searched the covers for a while before the sheets and still came up empty. Pressing down on the top mattress, she could still feel the lump. It made the once soft tower hard and unbearable. All this time they had teased her over it and now she knew something was in her mattress or under it or...

"What the hell is protruding into me?" Snorting, she began searching between mattresses and box spring until at last her hand grazed against something cold.

41

She froze. *What is that?*

Her hand wiggled back to it, pushing her arm deeper between the two mattresses. Again, her fingers found something cold and metallic. She gripped it and yanked it out. Turning on her nightstand lamp she looked closer. The top was adorned with a jeweled disc and as she unfolded her fingers, it became noticeably clear what the metallic item was meant for.

"Is this... is this a butt plug?" She shook her head, wondering where it came from. "Did someone come in here and fuck on my bed? Without me? No, no... this is new. This was hidden inside my bed. But why? And by who?"

She weaseled back onto the bed and marveled over the jeweled item. Part of her wondered if they were real crystals at the way they sparkled in the lamp light. She grinned. I *will put this item into good use for disrupting my orgasm.*

Hands snaked between her thighs. She dipped the plug into her wet pussy, before sliding further down. The plug slid inside her ass until it crested over the widest part and stopped at the disc. She moaned as her fingers glided back to her clit and began circling. The added pleasure of the plug made her peak faster than expected and she lunged forward as she came.

"If only I had a cock or dildo..." Panting for a moment, she rolled out of bed in frustration. "Dammit, that wasn't completely satisfying enough. Where's my phone?"

Looking to her nightstand it was gone. Startled, she rushed to the bar but saw no signs there. She spun back to the kitchen. Relief washed over her to see it on the counter. The screen read, *1 unread message.* Sighing, she unlocked it to see where Michael had sent her a single text:

[Mikey: I'm gone. Door's locked. Sleep well, Princess Pea.]

[Pearl: Thanks. Having a hard time sleeping.]

She eyed the fridge. The idea of eating some cherries without anyone here to see her mess proved tempting. The phone buzzed, slowing her as she sashayed across her kitchen, still nude as she gripped the fridge door. She couldn't stop smiling. Her night had taken an interesting turn.

The phone buzzed once more, and she snorted at the text.

[Mikey: You're still awake! Why would you still be awake?]

How nosy of you! Or...are you calling me out over that conversation, you ham.

[Pearl: There was a lump in the mattress.]

[Mikey: Princess Pea! I knew it!]

[Pearl: Stop calling me that!]

[Mikey: So did you figure out what the lump was?]

Opening the fridge, she paused, paling. The bowl of cherries sat there with a glass object mixed into them. Pulling the bowl out, she hesitated to pull the glass object out.

Walking to the counter, she studied the artful glass... stick. *Didn't Chuckles cover these with plastic wrap?*

She took in the cherry décor, like a ball sack on a long glass stick with red ribbing spiraling into the cherries. The tip and overall shape phallic and unmistakable. This was another object left for her to discover. Looking back into the fridge, there was a notecard, one from her own office stationary.

The calligraphy within it made her blink twice, the handwriting artful as the object itself. It simply said: *Enjoy the birthday treasures.*

45

She stiffened, thinking of the butt plug prompted her to pull the glass stick from the bowl. The end of it curved upward and she bit her bottom lip.

This couldn't be... do they make dildos in glass? I've never seen one like...

Her phone buzzed again, bringing her attention to it.

[Axel: Just let me know if you want me to return tonight and give you a hand ⊠]

Rolling her eyes, she returned to her messages, but another text interrupted.

[Gaston: I haven't given you your birthday gift yet. The cherry stem was a hint.]

This time, she covered her face. She had imagined what he could do with that tongue in all the right places. Shaking it off, she returned to her text chain with Michael. Him calling her out on the toys earned the prude the new bombardment of sexual treasures she had discovered.

[Pearl: Yeah. A butt plug. And now this in my cherries... *Picture of glass dildo*]

There was a long pause before the indicator signaled him responding. She snorted to herself, giggling. *I wonder what he will say?*

[Mikey: Sexy. Butt plug and a glass dildo. Nice buys, did Axel get those for you?]

I knew it! It is a glass dildo! Holy shit!

Looking back to the notecard, she snapped a photo and sent it to him.

[Pearl: No idea. They left me a note. You think I'll find more fun toys in my apartment?]

[Mikey: I can come over and help look. Please tell me you plan on using them.]

[Pearl: For a prude, you're rather pervy tonight.]

47

[Mikey: You just assume I'm a prude. Don't forget, I'm friends with Axel, Princess Pea. Birds of a feather flock together... or fuck together? Not sure if that sounds as well as it did in my head. LOL]

[Pearl: LMAO]

Pearl shoved the phone aside, plucking a cherry from the bowl. Scanning her apartment, her curiosity and excitement grew. The glass dildo was far too cold to play with just yet. Looking around the kitchen, she picked apart everything. At last, she did a double take on an item in her utensil cup. Something seemed new, longer than the others.

Picking up another cherry, she marched over to the bin and flipped on the kitchen light. "Wow... that's not what I thought that was..." The leather utensil was a riding crop, making her cheeks red. "I don't think I've ever done any spanking with anyone. Oh man, what if these are from Gaston?"

She laid the crop beside the glass dildo. Taking another photo, she was eager to send the latest report to Michael, enjoying the thought of torturing her friend.

Revenge for denying me to figure out that tongue piercing!

[Pearl: See, I can find them all on my own. *Picture*]

[Mikey: Well, well! And who gets to be on the receiving end of that little toy? You or him?]

[Pearl: No idea. I suppose it depends which *him* these are from.]

[Mikey: Oh? Do you have any guesses on who left them?]

[Pearl: Not yet. Though, Gaston doesn't seem farfetched at this point...]

Walking over to the hallway, she flipped on the lights for the living room and bar. Something caught her eye in the blender. She looked back to her kitchen, scanning the area one more time before moving to the bar top. Moving around the counter, she approached the blender. They hadn't used it tonight, sticking to liquor, beer, and simple cocktails.

[Mikey: Still searching?]

She snorted at his text, ignoring it. Opening the lid to the blender, she dipped her fingers in to retrieve the shiny object. Much to her surprise, it was a magic bullet, the same brand and make of the vibrator Axel had used on her time and time again.

A shudder of anticipation rattled her shoulders, her nipples erect thinking of it. She snapped another photo on the kitchen counter, her collection of toys growing quickly.

[Pearl: Score! *Picture*]

[Mikey: I take it you're familiar with this one?]

[Pearl: Indeed, Mr. Prude. A personal favorite.]

[Mikey: Well, at least you have your own now. Any idea who's left you these little treasures yet, Princess?]

[Pearl: Maybe Axel? I mean, this is the same one he has. And he did text, asking to give me a hand.]

[Mikey: You could always ask.]

[Pearl: I'm not asking. What if I guess the wrong person?]

[Mikey: Smart girl. You should keep looking. I'm sure they've left you a good hint on their identity.]

Gaston is definitely dominate whip type. Though, I don't think Axel owns anything similar in his own collection. In fact, I'm a little conflictive about it being either of them at this stage.

5

Treasures

Heaving a sigh, Pearl sat at the kitchen counter, snacking on cherries. She reviewed her thoughts, separating the items. Gaston and Axel both had lingered here, perhaps the toys were left from both. Shaking her head, it begged the question of when either of them had a moment to slip into her room during the party unnoticed.

I locked my bedroom door when the guests started to arrive, I'm sure of it. So, who left the butt plug?

Picking up the glass dildo with the cherry design, this came from someone who knew she loved cherries. Her mind circled back to Chuckles, but they had just met. There was no way some dorky catering guy would hide erotic gifts in her apartment with such decisive locations. Besides, she had watched him put them away earlier with plastic wrap, so someone followed behind him to place the dildo and note in the fridge.

It had to be someone who has been over here. So that rules out... Gaston. That man isn't as romantic as he makes himself out to be. He's just a beast of sexual prowess and dominance.

Looking at the magic bullet, she smirked. "And I don't think Axel got me this. He's not one to invest in a friend-with-benefits. Hell, he didn't get his girlfriend a gift for her birthday after a year together."

Pearl hummed to herself, walking through her apartment like a nude phantom. She flipped on the lights, peered into vases, drawers, checked under couch cushions. Everything she had found was close to the kitchen and bedroom. Circling back, she double checked the fridge and freezer. *Nothing.* Opening and closing every drawer and cabinet, she snacked on a few cherries in thought. Her phone buzzed.

[Gaston: You still up?]

[Pearl: You can say that.]

[Gaston: I can circle back, tucker you out.]

Rolling her eyes, she was quick.

[Pearl: I'll take a rain check. Trying to figure out who left some items at my apartment.]

This should reveal if it's him.

[Gaston: Oh no. Did someone forget their wallet?]

Sucking on a cherry, she arched an eyebrow. *Nope.*

[Pearl: Yeah, waiting to hear back now.]

[Gaston: Another time?]

Pearl started to respond but deleted the *maybe.* Changing course, she decided to try the same verbiage and see what response she could muster from Axel. Putting Gaston on silent, she moved on to suspect number two.

[Pearl: Did you leave something at my apartment?]

There was a long pause and she waited with patience. The cherries had stained her lips and fingers red, but she didn't care. They were in peak season and sweet on her tongue. The earthy after tone was something she couldn't resist.

Her phone buzzed.

[Axel: No. I got my wallet and phone. Keys on the nightstand. Why?]

[Pearl: Were you asleep already?]

[Axel: Yeah.]

[Pearl: Good night, Axel. I'll find the owner eventually.]

She grabbed another cherry, sucking on it. Staring at her phone, she scrolled through her contacts, reviewing her party guest list. Very few of her past conquests were in attendance, but no one seemed bold enough to leave the smattering of sex toys. She wiggled; very aware she hadn't removed the bejeweled butt plug during the scavenger hunt.

[Mikey: Found anything else?]

No! Her eyes grew wide. *It couldn't be.*

[Pearl: I'm still searching.]

She paused, covering her mouth.

That kiss. Those stolen looks. Could it be he had something far bigger planned for me tonight? With him?

[Mikey: Need me to come over and help?]

Pearl bit into the next cherry, a grin on her face. Goosebumps rippled over her body.

[Pearl: Where should I look next?]

[Mikey: The bar. There's more to be found, I'm sure of it.]

Of course, you are! Suspect number three!

Leaving the kitchen island, she marched back to the bar area. Her eyes fell on something purple on two of the liquor bottles. She rounded the counter and plucked them from the bottles. The two purple silicone items were new and foreign to her. She twirled them in her fingers as she returned to the kitchen where her pile of treasures sat.

A spark of arousal sent a chill up her spine, *these were left for me.*

[Mikey: Well? Turn up anything, Princess Pea?]

He was the last one to touch the bar. I help him finish and everyone had left. Mikey... the prude... he's the mystery man who left me my treasures. He was here long before I even got home from work, he had plenty of time to hide the butt plug under the mattress and considering his nickname for me...

[Pearl: Enlighten me, oh prude bartender. What on earth would one do with these? *Picture of purple mystery item*]

[Mikey: Well that's for this... *Picture of a nipple on a hard plane, tattooed pec*]

Pearl sat down, choking on a cherry. She hadn't expected a picture. Picking up the purple bulb and it became evident these suctioned to the nipples, easily keeping a tight seal. She licked her lips, staring at her phone.

A naughty thought trickled forward, her heart racing at the idea. *Do I dare meet tit for tat? Would he be willing to return tonight and...*

[Pearl: Like so? *Close up of a covered nipple with the purple sucker*]

[Mikey: Wait for it...]

Wait for what?

She furrowed her brow, then... *gasped.*

The purple started to fade into hot pink as the silicone heated to her body temperature. Pearl covered her face. She didn't know if this added to how ridiculous she felt, but there was no denying, he had left her the grand display of toys.

Gathering them into a pile again, she took a photo and sent it his way.

[Pearl: Cute! Now, was this everything? *Picture*]

[Mikey: I don't see the butt plug.]

[Pearl: You'll have to come over to see that one.]

Let's see how far you're willing to go, Michael. Was this just for kicks, or were you hoping to come into my bedroom with me?

[Mikey: Okay. I went home to shower and change. Grabbing the keys now. Should I just walk in? Or knock?]

[Pearl: You got keys to the castle. Come show this Princess how the Prince does business.]

[Mikey: ⊠ You ever been licked by this? *Picture of tongue with two inline piercings*]

[Pearl: I got kissed by that today and it was pretty impressive.]

[Mikey: Send me a shot of you playing with your toys.]

So bold!

Pearl felt the heat rising in her cheeks.

Why am I feeling bashful? Is it because I've never sexted with toys? Or is it just intimidating because I'm doing this with Michael, out of all guys?

[Pearl: Aren't you driving?]

[Mikey: Nope. Gubering so I can play along. *Picture of an uncovered forearm revealing tattoos of black and gray koi fish and lotus pond*]

Tattoos! I mean I've noticed some peeking out on occasion of his sleeves and a few times he rolled up a sleeve, but wow! That's some serious ink. Didn't take him for tattoo and piercing type of guy. What the hell? I've known him five years and never once did he ever say anything. To say you're a private man is an understatement.

[Pearl: Okay, how's this. *Picture of breasts, one purple and one pink nipple sucker*]

[Mikey: You crack me up. A little uneven there. Granted, so am I... *Picture of the other forearm with scars and tattoos fighting for space?*]

61

Oh no... those scars... is this why...

Tears welled up in her eyes. All the teasing and she never knew. This whole time, always rolling up the single sleeve and keeping his shirt on, without a doubt, returned to this one factor. The pieces were falling together with the passing on beach days and the likes.

Dammit. I feel like an utter bitch.

[Mikey: Stop feeling sorry for me. They couldn't cover these, the rest you can't see anymore.]

[Pearl: I'm such a dumbass.]

[Mikey: Send me nudes then. :p I still have half an hour to play! Stop stalling!]

Pearl laughed, shaking her head. He never once took it personal. Just accepted it as friendly razzing. Scooping up all the toys, she scurried back to her bed with all her new treasures laid out before her. Picking up the glass cherry dildo, she bit her lip.

I think I know how I can make this up to him.

Climbing onto the four-post bed, mattresses stacked high enough to make her feel small as she pulled onto it. Readjusting all her pillows, she propped herself up. The lamp lit the area well, casting hard shadows in all the right places. Positioning the camera, legs straddled, the butt plug sparkled from its resting place and the light gave away how wet she had become.

Snapping a photo, she sent it.

[Pearl: Here's the butt plug *Picture of wet pussy and sparkling butt plug*]

[Mikey: Glad you like it. That one wasn't cheap.]

She paled, the thought snaking back to the surface, *are those real crystals?*

[Pearl: You can't be serious! These are real crystals?]

[Mikey: Only the best for my Princess Pea. Now, show me more.]

So, demanding... and to think, he'll be here soon, and all his secrets will be revealed. I can't get my heart to stop racing. I'm nervous, like the first time all over again and well, I can't lie, this isn't what I had in mind nor who I thought I would fuck this week. Michael knows how to throw a girl a birthday party. Showered me with amazing treasures and riding over to join. That's sexy on a lot of levels.

Playful

Grabbing the lube from the nightstand, she couldn't deny her growing desire and arousal to play with herself. By the time Michael would get here, she might orgasm a few times. She dribbled the lube onto the glass dildo, curious what such a hard and ribbed object might feel like against the soft heat of her pussy. She slid it in, slow at first. The glass cool in comparison, making her tense and adding to the pleasurable sensation of the ribbing. At last, it was in until it looked like a set of glass cherries sitting atop her pussy. She snapped a photo.

[Pearl: I don't think I can eat these cherries *Picture*]

[Mikey: No, but don't worry. I'll clean up the juice they make. Starting to get hard. Send more. *Picture of the tent in his pants*]

[Pearl: So, how big are you compared to this little treasure? *Picture of the glass dildo almost all the way out, wet and sparkling*]

[Mikey: What do you think? *Picture of his dick, hard and erect, taller than his hand and thick even in his own grip*]

Pearl paused, glaring at the photo for a moment. Sure, she had been sent plenty of dick pics, but not built like this. This one was worthy of keeping saved in the hidden folders of her phone for later. She had been with someone with length, but not with the girth she could see in the photo. Her mind recalled how he gripped the bottle tops and spouts. He was no doubt thicker.

Shit, I think he might be the biggest cock I've been with! Happy birthday me!

[Mikey: Not very often I get to render you speechless >:}~ *Another shot of his cock with precum dribbling from the tip*]

[Pearl: You're putting your treasures to shame with that thing... *Picture of the dildo halfway inside her pussy*]

[Mikey: I want to be there *Picture of him making a sad face*]

[Pearl: Too bad *Picture of her sticking her tongue out*]

[Mikey: Almost there. Had to tuck it away before I scarred the Guber driver. Granted, it's Chuckles so...]

[Pearl: Stop it!!! LOL]

Pulling off the nipple suckers, she pushed her breast together and snapped a shot. She took a moment to admire how erect and swollen her nipples had become. The dusky pink now a rosy red like a cherry, seemed appropriate for the way her night seemed to unfold. With a toothy grin, she sent the photo.

[Pearl: The girls needed to breathe *picture*]

[Mikey: You think my cock would fit between them?]

[Pearl: I was wondering if it would fit in my pussy as it is LOL]

[Mikey: Don't tell me I'll be your biggest????]

[Pearl: Definitely the thickest...]

There was a long pause. Pearl puffed out her cheeks. No signs of him writing and panic began building as her anxiety stung her chest.

Covering her face, she dreaded she had sent the words.

Why the hell the wave of honesty? What's wrong with me!

Looking down at her phone, there wasn't any signs of a response. She flopped back into her pile of pillows, groaning. Scrolling back over the exchange of photos and words, she paused on the cock shots. Reaching over for the glass dildo, she began sliding it in and out, imagining a cock filling all the space her new toy couldn't fathom to compete with.

Who knew he was packing something this monstrous in those high thread count khakis. And to think, its mine tonight, but I'm nervous. We've been friends for so long and those scars.

Swiping she lingered on the photo, the ink looking fresher in comparison to the other arm. Blinking she became curious and compared the two arms. These were done at various times, usually are, but the scarred arm is definitely recently healed with as dark as the ink held and it seemed to have a hint of lotion or ointment on it.

Was that why he had to go home? Granted, he showed up in that bartending outfit and worked like that all night. Kind of cute he would rush home to clean up and return. I had a shower, but did he want to see how I would react to the toys? Maybe he thought I would discover them in the morning and didn't want to push his luck.

Scrolling back to the dick pics, she bit her lip. Her body throbbed with want. It made her anxious, but it stirred a level of desire she hadn't felt in some time. Tonight would be more than a one nightstand or friend with benefits hookup. If she knew anything about Michael or from that kiss, he intended to take his time with her.

He's so thick, even when holding his own cock. How hard it must get just before he starts to...

70

Swallowing, she arched, the dildo rubbing against a new area. Her climax was starting to rise and she would peak soon. The more her body squeezed around the glass dildo the more pleasurable the ribbing became. Her breath caught with her rising excitement. Eyes heavy lidded as they took in the photo of his raging hardon, fueling her to thrust the dildo faster.

She turned her wrist, the rubbing tweaking to a new spot. Another swift inhale, moaning as she arched.

"Well, well..." Michael's voice jolted her.

Dropping the phone, it smacked her in the face. "Ouch!"

"Shit!" He rushed the bed, pulling the phone off her face before she could. "That had to hurt." He glanced at the screen and smirked. "It's thick, hard, and heavy when hitting you in the face like that."

"Stop it," she looked away, but his hand pulled her chin back to him.

Michael's lips pressed against hers, rolling his tongue piercing against her own tongue. Both piercings became very clear. The heat of his hand glided over her abdomen and cupped her own hand while still gripping the glass dildo. He began guiding her movements, deepening the kiss and inviting her into his own mouth. The scent of him excited her, freshly showered and a spritz of his alluring cologne goading her sexual tide to peak.

He twisted the glass dildo and rubbed the angled tip downward. This made a new sensation as her pussy tightened in response as the butt plug became part of the playful stroking. His other hand snaked between them, massaging her breast, his thumb circling her nipple. She arched and he broke the kiss to hear her moan. Her bottom lip trembled, teetering on the edge of an orgasm.

Hot lips wrapped around her nipple and she whimpered. He suckled, hungry to taste her flesh before rolling his piercings over the swollen flesh. Another turn of the wrist and he found a spot she had neglected, his thrusting of the dildo faster, firmer. She arched and tried to muffle the scream by biting her lip. He released her nipple with a pop, the wetness he left behind still adding to her arousal.

"Don't hold back. I want to hear you scream." His breath tickled at her ear as he whispered in that suave tone. "I don't give a fuck if you call out someone else's name, just let me show you who I am behind closed doors tonight."

Pearl's eyes were shut tight, the pleasure peaking as his tongue teased her nipple, lips daring to wrap around it once more. The orgasm exploded and she tried the lunge forward. Michael abandoned his play. The glass dildo was quickly replaced with two thrusting fingers and his lips now ensnared her swollen clit. She folded over him, thighs shaking as she came hard. The gush of fluid confirming he had taken her above what she had aimed to do alone.

"Fuck yes!" she cried. "Don't stop, Mikey... Don't..."

Her hands wrapped around his head, grinding in him as she shrieked in delight. The *bump, bump* sensation of his piercings added fuel to the erotic fire he had set ablaze throughout her entire being. When at last the edge slowed and he pulled away from her, she was left breathless. He turned away, stepping just out of the light of her lamp as he pulled his shirt off. Wiping her juice from his face with his shirt, he dropped it to the floor.

The muscles on this man... Axle... he's stacked and not even going to the gym every time!

7

Mystery
Man Revealed

It took a few blinks before Pearl's eyes settled on the artful tattoos etched into his back. The black and white work of art painted every inch of his skin like a full body suit. His pants slid to the floor, the ink never stopping as it flowed over his ass cheeks and down both legs. There were hints of scarring under them as the light hit him. Even the tattoos couldn't completely take them away, but the artwork did well to distract from it all.

A walking canvas and its... gorgeous.

A white crane stood in a bed of lotus, among a flurry of rushing waters and koi as if they lived and thrived on his skin. She propped herself up, eyes wide as she took in the details and marveled over the landscape painted on his chiseled frame. *Hours,* came to mind as to how long it must have taken to cover so much of his skin.

At last, he turned; a puppy dog look on his face softening his features as if unsure of her reaction.

Why is he so worried?

Across the front of his body, Koi fish seemed to battle for space, waves splashing up and over his ribs and shoulders. Her eyes chased the flow of the water down to where he stroked his huge cock, a condom already rolled on and ready for her. She held her breath. That and his hands were the only things she couldn't see signs of having a trace of ink. Again, much like the backside, the water with its koi and flowers spilled over his hips and down his legs, filling his flesh in an amazing form of living artwork.

Is it wrong I'm more excited to be fucked by such a work of art?

When Pearl broke from her gawking, she met his eyes and he waited to see her response. She broke into a smile, fading the tension in his shoulders. Michael had wanted her to see him in the low lighting first. With a few strides forward, the inked skin looked more magnificent. The gray washed shading artfully applied and the rigid line work, bringing depth to the living creatures swimming across the hard planes of muscles.

Her fingers reached out to touch his abdomen and he grabbed her wrist in panic.

"What's wrong?" Pearl's heart raced.

"If you do that, you'll feel them," he mumbled.

"The scars?" she questioned. "It's okay..."

Swallowing, he pressed her palm against his skin and goosebumps rippled over his skin. Pearl furrowed her brow, the bumps, and snags humbling. He had turned away, looking to nowhere while she traced one line up the center of his torso. She inhaled swift. In her lifetime, she had only seen scars like this once, on her father when they had to crack him open for emergency surgery.

Pearl scrambled to her knees, almost making her a little taller than him as he stood beside her bed. "Look at me," she demanded, cupping his face.

"So now you know my secret." There was pain in those eyes. "I was in a bad car crash when I was younger. They had to crack me open, and by some good fortune, they were able to save me. It's the reason for the crane," he shrugged, darting his eyes away from her. "I've spent years getting this ink done, attempting to cover them, but my arm..." Michael lifted the forearm. "It proved too stubborn I suppose."

Pearl kissed him on the lips, but before he could deepen the kiss, she began trailing kisses down his neck. She chose her path well, aiming to battle his wave of insecurities. In this fleeting moment together, everything he'd shown her made her fall in love with him. Trailing across his collarbone, he lips met the top of the scar that ran down his entire torso. He tensed under her touch, holding his breath. She was gentle as she kissed and licked the scar all the way down until at last, she licked the tip of his cock.

HA! A cherry flavored condom! We planned for everything!

By this point, he had taken a breath, his heart thudding fast and hard to the point where she could feel his pulse race under her every touch. Taking his cock into her mouth, she ached to give him enough space as to not nick him with her teeth. She sucked hard and long, sliding his hardened length in and out. Michael moaned, gripping her hair as he began to rock his hips. He cock pressed against the back of her throat and she encouraged him to stay as she shook her head. Another moaned rolled from him before she pulled back and off to inhale for air.

Before she could continue, he stopped her, flipping her onto her back and pulling her pussy to him. He pushed inside her wet heat, slow and a little at a time. She white knuckled the sheets at her sides, tensing at what was to come. He pressed further and further as they watched one another.

Pearl started moaning as he neared entering her all the way and stopped.

"So tight," he breathed, his cock throbbing inside.

"It feels... amazing." She reached down, fingers exploring the thick base of his dick entering her.

"Oh, let's not let this go to waste." He leaned over and made her gasp. "I charged it."

He wiggled the magic bullet and she paled.

"What's that expression?" He flipped it on, and her pussy tightened. "Oh, nervous, are we?"

"Michael, that's a bit much. You're pushing me over the edge," she warned.

He lowered the vibrating bullet, putting it dangerously close to her clit. "I'm pretty sure that was the goal of all these treasures I left you, Princess Pea."

"Mikey..." She looked at him, and he smirked.

The bullet moved down and met its target. She arched, squealing. Her body was electrified with vivid pleasure. Every part of her tensed, an orgasm peaking fast and hard. Another gush

81

and her pussy pulsed around his hard cock. He began grinding in and out, the bullet on its target and unmoving. Her scream heightened, the pleasure making her eyes roll back as he picked up speed.

At last, she couldn't stand it. His cock was growing stiffer and only intensified the erotic pleasure taking hold of her every fiber. She reached down, pulling his hands and the bullet away. He tossed it aside, moaning as he wrapped his arms under her. Pearl wrapped her arms around him, nails digging into this back, only goading him to fuck her slower. Michael would shove forward with great speed and pull back slow, making her arch into his body. Sweat coated her skin and his own, both lingering on the edge of an orgasm.

"Please..." she panted.

"Please?" His breath was hot across her ear and neck. "Are you begging for me to cum?"

"Please... cum for me." She felt his dick jerk inside her. "Michael, please fuck me faster, please cum for me, baby."

"Oh you're mean," he grumbled, arching enough to latch onto a nipple.

She tightened, moaning as she hugged his head into her breast. "Cum for me. Please...I can't... take it anymore."

He caved to her begging, pushing hard and fast, his huge cock unable to deny the tight heat of her pussy. She had gushed until both their thighs were slick and sheets a puddle. He had enjoyed it and at last moaned into her breast, nipple caught in his teeth as he shoved hard. The pulsing, rock-hard cock sent her moaning as she grinded against him, making his own linger longer than he had expected. He released her breast, moaning with heavy lidded eyes. At last they sat still, his cock still inside her pussy. Their gazes met and they both laughed.

"Why haven't we done this sooner?" he asked.

"You shouldn't have waited five years to remove your shirt, Prince Prude," she retorted.

Looking down between them, he pulled his dick from her and frowned, tossing the condom in a small waste basket. "Oh man..."

Pearl's heart jolted. "What's wrong? Did it break?"

"No, no... condom's fine, but..." He smirked, his fingers trailing across her clit, wet opening, and tapped on the butt plug. "We didn't get to pull the plug."

She laughed, laying back as she threw an arm over her face.

"Maybe after we take a short nap?" He crawled onto the bed, pulled her into him and massaging a breast.

"Didn't Axel tell you?" she teased.

84

"Honestly, I don't recall him spilling the beans about anal." He nuzzled her neck and shoulder before kissing it.

"He hates anal," she announced.

He pressed his chin on her shoulder. "No joke."

She cupped her hand where his squeezed her breast. "But I love it. Do you really need a nap to recoup?"

"You'll have to wait a bit... it takes some... what am I laying on?" Grunting, Michael reached back to pull something out from under him.

After a moment, he reveals the riding crop.

"By the way, was that for you or me?" Pearl takes it from him, both giggling over it.

"It depends. Who's doing the riding."

THE END

Honey Cummings

A passionate, award-winning author of Fantasy, Honey has turned her aim towards erotica. Blending everyday scenarios and crafting them into steamy, blood-boiling moments for every shade of audience. Whether you want something short and hot like a student-teacher hook up to the more paranormal flair where Sleep with Sasquatch has unexpected bonus, look forward to erotic short stories, novellas, and hopefully a Trilogy in the future. Honey's debut erotic short landed No. 3 in Urban Erotica and continues to satisfy readers time and time again. Be sure to leave her a review and let her know what you think!

MORE HONEY CUMMINGS BOOKS

Sleeping with Sasquatch
Cuddling with Chupacabra
Naked with New Jersey Devil
Laying with the Lady in Blue
Wanton Woman in White
Beating it with Bloody Mary

Beau and Professor Bestialora
The Goat's Gruff
Goldie and Her Three Beards
Pied Piper's Pipe
Princess Pea's Bed
Jack's Beanstalk

4 HORSEMEN PUBLICATIONS
EROTICA

DALIA LANCE
My Home on Whore Island
Slumming It on Slut Street
Training of the Tramp

72% Match
It Was Meant to be... Or Whatever

ALI WHIPPE

Office Hours
Tutoring Center
Athletics
Extra Credit

Bound for Release
Fetish Circuit
Now You See Me

4HORSEMENPUBLICATIONS.COM

www.ingramcontent.com/pod-product-compliance
Lightning Source LLC
Chambersburg PA
CBHW030215130726
47898CB00012B/1031